The Great Missing Flag Caper!

Spirit of America

Book #4

Other Books in this series:

The Great Missing Flag Caper!

For Ava ♡

Author: MaryTherese Grabowski
Illustrator: Michelle Graham Fricks

P.O. Box 3687
Cleburne, TX 76033

Copyright © 2017
Mary Therese Grabowski & Michelle Graham Fricks
Library of Congress Control Number:
Version 1.0

Paperback:
ISBN-10: 1-62080-087-X
ISBN-13: 978-1-62080-087-4

eBook:
ISBN-10: 1-62080-088-8
ISBN-13: 978-1-62080-088-1

For my husband, retired Air Force Colonel Bob Griffin:

Thank YOU for YOUR service and for protecting Old Glory.

The dedication of our U.S. Military is unwavering. Yours, my love, is exceptional. You make me a better American.

"I AM SOOOOOO EXCITED that I am the one who got picked to raise and lower the flag on the big flagpole at the front of my school," said a smiling America to her mom at breakfast.

What an amazing day today will be. America Johnson is FINALLY going to be part of the flag raising detail at her school.

"This is absolutely an honor! Remember to treat the flag with respect at all times," said Mrs. Johnson. "Oh, I will mom, don't you worry," America assured her mom as she gathered her books and scurried off to school.

"Hey Elisa, wait up", yelled America as she ran to catch up with her very best friend in the whole world Elisa Martinez. America and Elisa met in pre-school when Elisa's family moved to the United States from Mexico because her Dad began working for a new company.

"Are you ready for your new job raising and lowering the flag?" asked Elisa. "You know it!" America replied. "I'll tell you ALL about it when I get to class. I am so excited. Mrs. Alexander in the office says I have to go through a quick lesson on the Stars and Stripes."

"What are the stars and stripes?" asked Elisa. "Oh, that's the traditional nickname for the Flag of the United States." America explained, "You can even call it Old Glory or The Star Spangled Banner." "Wow! All those names for the flag?" asked Elisa in amazement. "Uh huh... but wait... there's more!" America confidently said to her friend.

As they continued along walking to school the detailed information flowed from America. "Did YOU know Betsy Ross from Philadelphia made the original flag in 1776? It had thirteen white stars on a blue field. "Neat! I hadn't heard that," Elisa said. America wasn't finished with her history lesson for Elisa. "Those thirteen white stars represented the thirteen original colonies in America. There were thirteen red and white stripes there too. The color red represented valor and bravery and white stood for purity and innocence. The blue field was for justice and vigilance."

"Wow, how do you know this stuff America? You are the perfect student to be part of this flag detail at school!" replied Elisa. America told her how she loves the history of our country and that the flag is the most patriotic symbol representing the U.S. "Our flag today has fifty stars, one for each state and the thirteen red and white stripes represent the thirteen original colonies."

"I think I will start calling you Miss Patriot" giggled Elisa to America. Rolling her eyes America reminded her "HELLO??? My name is AMERICA?! You can't get more patriotic than that!" They laughed and gabbed about Old Glory the entire way to school. When they arrived Elisa walked to her home room and America went straight to the office for her instructions before beginning her flag detail.

"Good Morning Mrs. Alexander I am reporting for flag duty!" America said proudly. "Come on in here America. I want to go over a few things with you and the other students who are working on this detail. You know Garrett, Allie, and Bradley don't you?" asked Mrs. Alexander as she led America behind the front desk to the other three students. "Oh yes, ma'am... hi, guys," America greeted. "First, I am very proud of each of you for wanting to be part of one of the finest traditions in our country and our school system. The raising and lower of the flag of our country is a true honor, but it has a lot of responsibility too," said Mrs. Alexander.

"What kind of responsibility?" asked Garrett.

"Well," explained Mrs. Alexander, "there must be absolute utmost respect for the flag. Did you all know there are actual laws that protect the U.S. Flag and those laws explain how to show respect to the flag?"

Bradley seemed puzzled and asked, "Do you mean there is a set of rules on how to treat the flag?"

"Absolutely," said Mrs. Alexander. "First, the flag must NEVER touch the ground or anything below it. It should always be held upright and high."

"I NEVER knew THAT! What else?" asked Garrett.

"You should never draw on an American Flag, wear it as clothing or use it in any manner that might bring disgrace to the country," Mrs. Alexander explained.

"Well I saw someone wearing a shirt made of the flag once, so you mean that was wrong?" asked Allie.

"Yes, you should never do that," said Mrs. Alexander, "And you should also remember that if you plan to fly the US flag after dark it must have a spotlight on it."

America chimed in, "That's why we take ours down at home at night because we DON'T have a spotlight for it yet."

"WOW! I felt that our flag was special, but I didn't realize it was THAT special with a whole set of rules."

"I can definitely follow those rules," said Allie. "When do we get started?"

"Well, before we assemble you four into a straight line to march the flag out front, we must get the flag from the closet over by Principal Cantrell's office," said Mrs. Alexander walking over to the closet.

When she opened the door to get the flag, the students heard her gasp!

"Oh my goodness! Where is it? The flag is gone!"

The only thing in the closet was a hanging sweater and two empty shelves.

"What do we do?" asked Bradley.

America immediately proclaimed "We will find that flag! It has to be around here somewhere."

Mrs. Alexander ushered the four off to class as the bell rang for school to begin.

"You all can search for the flag on recess and at lunch. I'm sure with teamwork we will get to the bottom of this," said Mrs. A.

The detail split up and headed to class. America was puzzled that the American Flag was missing. She looked so bothered that when Elisa saw her in class she asked,

"What's up, America? How was the flag detail?"

America whispered "We didn't do it. The flag is missing!"

"WHAT?" yelled Elisa out loud "The flag is missing?!"

Everyone turned and looked at America and Elisa.

"Was it stolen?" yelled one student.

"Did someone hide it?" asked another.

"I'm not sure, but we gotta find it," replied America.

"We'll help you search" whispered Elisa "But when do we start?"

"We start at recess in one hour. Everyone be thinking of places around the school to look," instructed America.

Their teacher couldn't help but notice the distraction among the students, they were not focusing on math but rather more on the plan to find the missing flag. An hour later the bell for recess rang.

"Ok everyone, what's on your mind? Where do you want to check?" asked America.

"How about the gym?" suggested one student.

That's where they started the search but unfortunately, the flag was not there, just a basketball net and someone's sneakers.

Then someone else yelled "What about the cafeteria? Maybe someone thought the flag would look good in there."

So, a check of the cafeteria was next. Just empty lunch tables could be seen. No American Flag in sight.

"We will find this flag if it's the last thing we do," said America. Everyone hurried back to class and tried again later during lunch. The students checked the library, the auditorium, and even the bathrooms! No one saw the American Flag. Now it was the end of the school day. America, Bradley, Allie and Garrett all met up in the office before leaving school to talk to Mrs. Alexander one last time. Allie asked "Mrs. A did you find the flag?" Mrs. Alexander answered, "No Allie, I was hoping one of you did." The students shrugged their shoulders and shook their heads no. America chimed in "We even had other students in our classes helping us. We looked everywhere and no one could find it." "You all gave it a good try. Come back here in the morning and we will start our search all over again," said Mrs. Alexander. **22**

On the way home, Elisa and America continued talking about the flag. "I just don't understand where that flag could be," America told Elisa. "I'm sure you will find it tomorrow, don't worry," said Elisa. "By the way, you mentioned the flag was also called the Star Spangled Banner... isn't that the name of a song too?" she asked. "Actually yes, you are right! Our National Anthem is also called the Star Spangled Banner because it is a song about The Flag of our country," said America. "And a man named Francis Scott Key wrote the song The Star Spangled Banner." "Ok, Miss Patriot... Thanks for the patriotic lessons today!" said Elisa with a smile.

23

The topic of discussion at the dinner table in the Johnson home that evening was the flag.

"Gee America, that's too bad about the missing flag," said her brother Sam.

America looked sad sitting with her chin propped on her hands waiting for her Mom to put dinner on the table.

"Come on America it will be ok, you'll find the flag, cheer up! Look, even Liberty is trying to make you smile" said Mr. Johnson, as their dog Liberty was on her hind legs wagging her tail.

"Ok Miss Liberty off you go, no pups at the table during dinner," said Mrs. Johnson as she brought America's favorite dinner to the table. "Mac and cheese for everybody!"

"I'm not hungry, Mom," said America.

"WOW!" yelled Sam, "She must really be sad to not want to eat mac and cheese!"

Mr. Johnson encouraged America to try to eat a little bit because it might help her think better about where the missing flag could be.

"Ok Dad, you're right," said America who smiled from ear to ear as she took her first bite of her mom's famous mac and cheese!

After dinner America called several of her friends on the phone to see if any of them had more ideas of where to hunt for Old Glory. No one had any new ideas, but they agreed they would meet up with America and the other 3 students on the flag detail in the morning to help create a bigger search party.

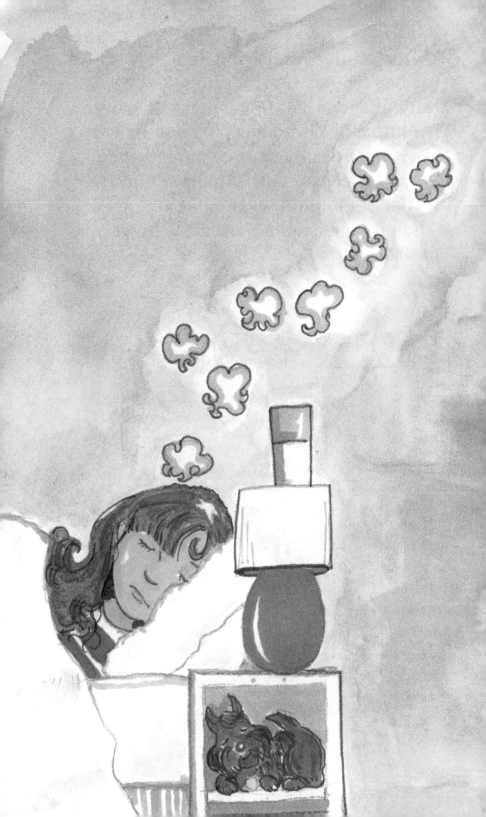

All night long America dreamed about raising the flag at school but the flag pole remained empty, even in her dreams.

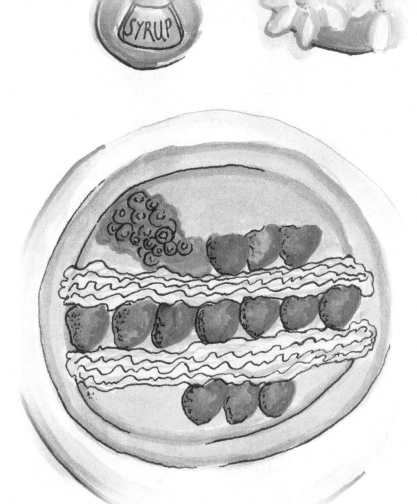

The next morning America's mom fixed patriotic pancakes to lift her spirits! "Thanks, mom! I love it when you put blueberries, strawberries and cream on the pancakes it makes them so good!" said America. "You are welcome! This should bring you good luck in your search for the flag this morning," replied Mrs. J.

They met up with about two dozen other students wanting to help find The Star Spangled Banner. When Principal Cantrell opened his office door and saw all the students there he was surprised!

"Wow, why are so many of you here in the office?" he asked.

America said "Well Sir, we're not sure how to tell you this but when we went to raise the flag yesterday it was gone! We have looked all over the school since yesterday morning and have had no luck.

So we decided to put an even bigger group together today to find it!"

Principal Cantrell grinned and said "Well, guess what? That won't be necessary because I HAVE OLD GLORY right here!"

"WHAAATT???! I don't understand The flag was gone yesterday, and no one had any idea where it had gone," said America.

"Actually, this is a new Flag. Apparently, the note I left explaining what I was doing was lost. I took the old one and had it properly disposed of at the local American Legion because it was faded from the weather and started to tear. You should NEVER fly an American Flag if it is weathered or torn. In fact, it is more respectful to have an empty flag pole until you get a brand new one to fly. So your great missing flag caper is solved, everyone!" All the students cheered and assembled outside to see the new flag take its first trip up the school flagpole. America briskly pulled the thin rope, one hand over the other, very steadily raising the flag with pride. She smiled a mile wide looking up as she placed her right hand over her heart once the flag reached the top of the pole.

"I PLEDGE ALLEGIANCE to the FLAG"

Once Old Glory reached the top of the flag pole a huge wind blew in and made her fly straight and beautiful for all to see. America and the students all recited:

"I Pledge Allegiance, to the Flag of the United States of America. And to the Republic for which it stands, One Nation, Under God, Indivisible, with Liberty and Justice for All."

America's Quiz

Who made the first flag?

Where was it made?

How many stars and stripes are on the original flag, and what colors were they?

How many stars and stripes are on the flag today?

What do the colors on the flag mean?

Name at least two nicknames for the flag.

What must a flag have on it if it flies at night?

The flag should never touch the what?

Should you fly a flag even if it is torn?

Recite the Pledge of Allegiance

Hello,
My Fellow Patriots!

Check on us often at
www.spiritofamericabooks.com
to see about our next patriotic
adventure! You can also connect
with us on Twitter and Facebook.

Find us on

MaryTherese (MT) Grabowski

doesn't just bleed red. Red, white and blue to be more precise! This only daughter of six children born into an Air Force family has a patriotic gene that has only strengthened with life experiences.

Grabowski's imagination gave her a passion for writing and storytelling. After graduation from Wesleyan College with a degree in Communications, Grabowski spent the next twenty years in broadcasting. First on the air in radio and then as a reporter and television news anchor. The military and government were two of this award winning journalists beats, so telling those stories not only honed her skills it made her passion for patriotism and writing to help keep people informed grow.

She was lured from the broadcast news business into the military advocacy world where she spent six years defending Robins AFB Georgia and our United States Air Force at the local, state and national levels as the Executive Director of a non-profit organization. It was during this time that something life changing happened. Her then 12 year old niece wanted to go to Washington DC on a trip. Grabowski told her niece that they would vacation to D.C. later in the year for a fun, but it would be an educational trip!

One day during the Presidential Campaign in 2008 Grabowski and Sam were listening to the radio in the car when a story came on about Barack Obama winning the Democratic Nomination. The news story was discussing who his potential cabinet members might be. Grabowski asked Sam, "Can you tell me who makes up The President's Cabinet?" Samantha without hesitation responded, "Why do I care who makes his furniture?" Needless to say Grabowski almost wrecked the car. This bright, well-educated niece was serious. Grabowski quickly learned that most students do not seriously learn about government until they are a sophomore in high school. To the author, that was alarming as in two years, students will be eligible to vote.

After a restless night of sleep, the character America Johnson and The Spirit of America Series was born.

Michelle Graham Fricks

Michelle Graham Fricks is an eccentric, passionate, magical thinker, and artist that has a diverse background. Another unique quality she possesses is that she remembers distinctly what it is like to be a kid.

She was a military kid, but not a typical one. She was taught patriotism and serving others early in life by her father, who is a Vietnam Veteran and further served through the Air National Guard and her mother who was, and still is, a talented homemaker. She is the oldest of three sisters, so there was always a lot going on in their house.

This did not stop Michelle from finding time to sit in her favorite persimmon tree so she could imagine and draw. Then in Kindergarten she heard many, many stories and listened to fairy tales on small records with the turn-along books. She admired the lovely art in those books so much, and loved when the teacher would turn the book to show the illustrations to the class.

Then, the teacher had the students write and illustrate their own books, and the drawings would no longer be called "drawings" but now "illustrations"! Her art mentor told her something very prophetic. He said, "One day, you will be illustrating for children, because your heart is so young. If you don't, it would be a shame." What a wise sage.

Michelle simply feels she is fulfilling her mentor's prediction. As patriotic as she is quirky, she wants to help our youngest citizens come to an understanding of our country's history and how it works today. She wishes to help etch it in a most engaging way, yet never forgetting that they are children that cannot wait for the teacher to turn the book around to show the picture to them.

CPSIA information can be obtained
at www.ICGtesting.com
Printed in the USA
BVOW11s1117150617
486957BV00002B/5/P